For Lucan Rocco Wood, my favourite beach companion – C.F.

For Marta and Natalia. And pirate girls everywhere – K.M.

PICTURE SQUIRRELS

Published in 2017 in Great Britain by Barrington Stoke Ltd
18 Walker Street, Edinburgh, EH3 7LP

www.picturesquirrels.co.uk

Title of the original German edition: *Käpten Knitterbart und seine Bande*
© 2003 Verlag Friedrich Oetinger GmbH, Hamburg

Illustrations © 2017 Kasia Matyjaszek
Translation © 2017 Barrington Stoke

A CIP catalogue record for this book is available
from the British Library upon request

ISBN 978-1-78112-692-9

Printed in China by Leo

Cornelia Funke   Kasia Matyjaszek

MOLLY ROGERS
PIRATE GIRL

PICTURE SQUIRRELS

Captain Firebeard was the terror of the high seas. His ship, the *Horrible Haddock*, sailed faster than the wind over the waves. Whenever the *Horrible Haddock* appeared on the horizon, the knees of honest sea-faring folk would shake like jelly.

Captain Firebeard had a fearsome crew. His helmsman was Morgan O'Meany. His cook was Cutlass Tom. Billy the Bald, William Wooden Hand, Crooked Carl and twenty more terrible pirates just like them made up the rest of the motley bunch.

When Captain Firebeard's crew boarded a ship, nothing was safe. They stole the silver spoons and the captain's uniform. They stole the ship's figurehead, the pots and pans, the hammocks and the sails. And, of course, they stole ALL the casks of rum.

But one day Captain Firebeard robbed a ship that he really should have left alone. On board was a little girl named Molly. Molly was off on a trip to see her grandma.

The pirates leaped on board with an ear-splitting roar. Molly tried hiding among the ropes, but Morgan O'Meany soon fished her out.

"What shall we do with her?" he said with a smirk.

"Take her with us, you fool!" Captain Firebeard bellowed. "Her parents will pay a handsome ransom for such a little treasure. And if not, then we'll feed her to the sharks."

"You'll be sorry for this!" Molly cried.

But Morgan O'Meany rolled her up like a herring and tossed her on board the *Horrible Haddock*.

When the sun had gone down, Billy the Bald dragged Molly to see the captain.

"All right, tell me your parents' names and address, or else!" Captain Firebeard growled.

"Will not!" Molly growled back. "If I told you my mother's name, you'd be so scared that you'd cry like a baby!"

At this, all the pirates howled with laughter.

So Molly was put to work. She peeled the potatoes and cleaned the boots. She polished cutlasses, patched sails and scrubbed the decks. Soon every bone in her body ached.

Three times a day Captain Firebeard asked her, "Name and address?"

But Molly just smiled.

"Feed her to the sharks!" roared William Wooden Hand.

But Captain Firebeard ground his teeth. "She'll talk before long," he said.

Every night the pirates had a party. They drank rum, staggered across the deck, danced on the ship's rigging and bawled out the rudest pirates' songs and sea shanties they knew.

One night the pirates partied until dawn. But this time they fell asleep on the deck.

Molly tiptoed over the tangle of arms and legs and threw a bottle over the ship's rail.

Splish! *Splash!* *Splosh!*

It landed in the deep, wide sea.

"Hey! What was that?" Morgan O'Meany yelled.

The pirates staggered over to the ship's rail.

"It's a message in a bottle!" they all cried.

"Bring it to me!" Captain Firebeard shouted. "Now!"

The pirates dived to the bottom of the sea. They searched and searched, but Molly's message in a bottle had bobbed away. They crawled back on deck, soaking wet and cursing.

"Tell me what you wrote!"
Captain Firebeard demanded.

But Molly just kicked at his
wooden leg.

Captain Firebeard turned
as red as a lobster. "NOW
it's time to feed her to the
sharks!" he roared.

But a cry from above stopped
him.

"P ... P ... P ... Pirates!" shouted
Ten-Pint Ted from the crow's
nest.

"Nonsense!" Captain Firebeard
scoffed. "*We're* the only
pirates around here."

But he was wrong. A ship with red sails was speeding towards them. A giant black flag with a skull and crossbones fluttered from its mast.

"Who in the name of Neptune's beard is that?" stuttered Captain Firebeard.

"That's my mum!" Molly grinned.

"It's Barbarous Bertha herself!" the crew of the *Horrible Haddock* wailed.

Captain Firebeard turned as white as a sheet and his pirates rolled their eyes in fear. This time it was *their* knees that were shaking.

Billy the Bald's false teeth almost flew out of his mouth.

The ship with the red sails drew closer and closer. Barbarous Bertha stood at the prow, swinging her cutlass.

"Wait until she sees my hands!" Molly said. "They're red and raw from peeling potatoes. That will make my mum maddest of all!"

Captain Firebeard and his pirates groaned with terror.

Soon Barbarous Bertha was alongside the *Horrible Haddock*. Her ferocious crew swung themselves over the rail with a terrible roar.

"We're here at last, my pirate girl!" Barbarous Bertha cried, and she threw Molly high into the air. "We got your message. Your grandma was beginning to wonder where you were. Now, how nasty can we be to these piratical nincompoops?"

"Well!" said Molly. "That's easy."

From that day on, Captain Firebeard and his pirate crew had no time to think about robbing ships.

William Wooden Hand scrubbed the deck.

Morgan O'Meany and Cutlass Tom peeled potatoes from morning until night.

Captain Firebeard polished Barbarous Bertha's boots fourteen times a week.

And at last Molly was able to visit her grandma!

Grow a love of reading

PICTURE SQUIRRELS